HOW TO RELEASE
A MISSIONAL MOVEMENT BY
DISCIPLING PEOPLE
LIKE JESUS DID

BUILDING A DISICPLING CULTURE

STUDY GUIDE

MIKE BREEN

Building A Discipling Culture: Study Guide
© Copyright 2020 by Mike Breen

Printed in the United States of America

Cover Design: Blake Berg
Layout Design: Jason Zastrow
Editors: Beccy Beresic, Sally Breen, Jason Zastrow, Robin Zastrow

ISBN: 978-0-9998981-1-6

3DM Publishing

3dmpublishing.com

CONTENTS

1

WHY DO WE USE LIFESHAPES?

Welcome to the *Building a Discipling Culture Study Guide!* We designed this guide to help you grasp, explore, and go deeper with the major concepts presented in *Building a Discipleship Culture.* The book was first published in 2005 and has gone on to become a global bestseller. Before diving in, we feel it's important to understand where and why this book was originally conceived. It came out of frustration and desperation that accompanied trying to disciple people who had little or no education, people who would traditionally never open a book and read it.

The following *LifeShapes* were designed to help those who had the least access to training yet wanted to grow in their understanding of Jesus and the Bible. The simplicity of the shapes allowed for easy understanding. The *LifeShapes* prevented the overwhelm and intimidation that can accompany text-centric methods. They could be shared on a napkin over coffee or a brown bag over lunch. You can read more about how our culture regularly communicates through shapes or memes in Chapter 5 of *Building a Discipling Culture* or in my book on communitcation, *Speak Out: Awakening Mission and Discipleship through Private and Public Communication.*

In this guide, we have attempted to make it again accessible and straightforward. It can be used by anyone, anywhere, and at any stage in their journey of faith. We pray that you will find many uses for this guide so that every disciple can be equipped in building a discipling culture in their homes, workplaces, school, and coffee shops.

Something of note before you begin: this study guide is not intended to be a leadership guide or a huddle companion. If you choose to use it that way, great! But it's best to be used in small groups, prayer triplets, house churches, or anywhere in between.

This guide does not go through *Building a Discipling Culture* exhaustively, but serves as a introduction through the key *LifeShapes*:

- The Matrix: Invitation & Challenge
- The Circle: Learning from Life
- The Triangle: Deeper Relationships
- The Semi-Circle: A Balanced Life
- The Square: Multiplying Life
- The Pentagon: Personal Calling
- The Hexagon: Definitive Prayer

It's our greatest joy to release this guide 32 years after *Building a Discipleship Culture* and the *LifeShapes* were conceived in the hard and desperate environment of the inner-city Brixton, UK where we poured ourselves out serving. Enjoy!

+M

2

THE MATRIX: INVITATION & CHALLENGE

Building a Discipling Culture: Chapters 1 & 2

How do we make disciples? Whether in the big or the small, in our everyday relationships or in our churches and denominations, the question of how we make disciples is at the core of every other question we ask in the church today. Which is as it should be since Jesus' commission to the church is to make and multiply disciples!

The church seems to be changing fast. What used to work isn't working any longer. While Christendom is crumbling around us, the call to make disciples still remains. In the wake of this crumbling, the church faces a discipleship problem. As leaders, our focus easily becomes on building the church ourselves, through all sorts of means of our own invention. But Jesus is the one who said he will build his church. Jesus' Plan A for building the church is discipleship. There is no Plan B.

How, then, does Jesus model discipleship? Jesus models discipleship through **invitation** and **challenge**.

Invitation is about being invited into a relationship where you have access to a person's life. Jesus' disciples had full access to him. Challenge is about the call to live into your identity as a son or daughter of the King. When accepting the invitation, you also accept the challenge that comes with it.

Is it that simple? Yes, it is that simple. Making disciples doesn't have to be complicated. However, that doesn't mean that discipleship isn't hard. Both invitation and challenge require intentional leadership.

Effective leadership means a leader invites disciples into relationship and challenges them to change. The interplay between invitation and challenge will influence the culture you lead. Lack of intentionality in both invitation and challenge leads to three different kinds of leadership cultures:

- Low invitation and low challenge leadership creates an **apathetic culture**. We call this **boring**.
- High invitation and low challenge leadership creates a **cozy culture**. We call **chaplaincy**.
- Low invitation and high challenge leadership creates a **discouraged culture**. We call this **stressful**.

Following Jesus' model, we can be intentional about balancing invitation and challenge: high invitation and high challenge leadership creates an **empowered culture**. We call this **discipleship**.

I use *The Invitation and Challenge Matrix* to help leaders understand the reality of the types of cultures we create in our churches.

THE MATRIX: INVITATION & CHALLENGE

THE MAIN IDEA:

Imitate Jesus' way of balancing invitation and challenge in your life and with those you lead.

HIGH INVITATION

CHAPLAINCY QUADRANT
Cozy Culture

DISCIPLING QUADRANT
Empowered Culture

LOW CHALLENGE

HIGH CHALLENGE

BORING QUADRANT
Apathetic Culture

STRESSFUL QUADRANT
Discouraged Culture

LOW INVITATION

BUILD THE MATRIX:

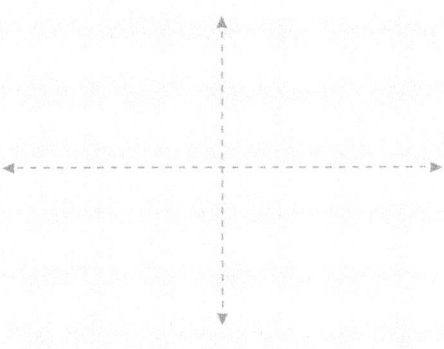

STUDY QUESTIONS

1. Define the following terms in your own words.

    Invitation:

    Challenge:

2. Give some examples of each invitation and challenge in Jesus' life and ministry.

    Invitation:

    Challenge:

3. Which are you more naturally inclined to be: invitational or challenging? How so?

4. Describe your current discipleship culture. Reflect upon which quadrant you might be in. Write down your reflections.

5. How might have you helped in creating the culture you described above?

6. What is something you can do to begin to balance both invitation and challenge?

3

THE CIRCLE: LEARNING FROM LIFE

Building a Discipling Culture: Chapter 6

The Circle represents our journey into the Kingdom of God. Mark 1:15 says, "The Time has come," [Jesus] said. "The Kingdom of God is near. Repent and believe the good news!" We experience the Kingdom of God through a process of repentance and belief initiated by a moment or event in time called a *kairos* moment.

Kairos is a Greek word meaning, "point in time, special event, or opportunity." When English speakers think of the word "time," they often think of the passing of time, from Point A to Point B. The Greek word for this type of time is *chronos*, from which we get the word chronology. Compared to this, *kairos* moments are "moments where time stands still." They can be positive or negative, recognized by the impact they leave on you and signal opportunities to grow.

As we encounter a *kairos* moment, God gives us the opportunity to repent and believe. Repent comes from the Greek word *metanoia*, which means "to have a change of mind and heart or reorientation." Believe comes from the Greek word *pistis*, which means, "to believe, trust," or more accurately, "to live as if what God is saying is true."

When we have a *kairos* moment, using *The Circle*, we are able to slow down and process through the moment and ask two key questions:

1. What is God saying to me?
2. What am I going to do about it?

The Circle is divided in half with repent on the right side, and believe on left side. Each side has three steps for a toal of six steps.

The three steps in the **repent** process include:

- Observe
- Reflect
- Discuss

The three steps in the **believe** process include:

- Plan
- Account
- Act

Once you are aware of *The Circle*, your life can look like a Slinky, a series of loops held together by time. Each time you go through the process of *The Circle*, that is each time you recognize a *kairos* moment and respond in repentance and belief, you grow a little more and take on a little more of the character of Christ.

Surrender to the process of change. Push through the pain of the internal struggle and you will taste the goodness of the Lord.

Go ahead! Use *The Circle* to learn from life.

THE CIRCLE: LEARNING FROM LIFE

THE MAIN IDEA:

As learners of Jesus, we choose to learn from life by observing how God is bringing the Kingdom of God near to us and then respond through repentance and belief.

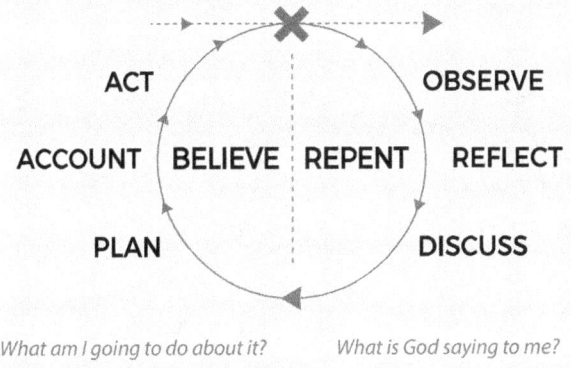

ACT				OBSERVE
ACCOUNT	BELIEVE	REPENT		REFLECT
PLAN				DISCUSS

What am I going to do about it?   *What is God saying to me?*

BUILD THE CIRCLE:

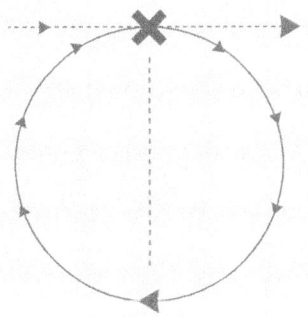

STUDY QUESTIONS

1. Define the following terms from Mark 1:15:

   Kingdom -

   Time (*kairos*) -

   Repent -

   Believe -

2. What are the three parts of the process for repentance? Defend why it is it important to slow down and be intentional about repentance.

3. What are the three parts of the process for belief? Defend why it is important to slow down and be intentional about belief.

4. Which of the six parts comes most easily? Which of the six parts of the Circle do you struggle with the most?

5. Identify a *kairos* moment from your life. Take the time to discuss it with others using the *Circle*.

4

THE TRIANGLE:
DEEPER RELATIONSHIPS

Building a Discipling Culture: Chapters 7 & 8

Being a disciple of Jesus means that we pattern our lives after the pattern he gives us. Jesus lived out his life in three-dimensional relationships:

Up—with his Father;

In—with his chosen followers;

Out—with the hurting world around him.

JESUS' UPWARD LIFE

Jesus was in constant contact with his Father, always speaking to him directly and speaking of him in personal, intimate, and familiar ways. Jesus did what he saw the Father doing and invited his disciples into the same type of relationship with the Father.

JESUS' INWARD LIFE

Jesus was always expanding the circle of those who he invited in. He designated the Twelve and invested into them in a unique way (just like a Huddle). Jesus "did life" with them.

JESUS' OUTWARD LIFE

Jesus knew he had a mission from the Father to live out, and he oriented everything he did around that mission — to reach out to a dark and dying world. Jesus did not wait for the spiritually dead to come to him; he went directly to them.

YOUR THREE-DIMENSIONAL LIFE

God created us for three-dimensional relationships, and when we lose sight of that, we live unbalanced lives. Churches can become Up and Inners, Up and Outers, or In and Outers. Be mindful of your church and any relational imbalance it might have.

So instead, walk with Jesus and invite him to be part of your everyday life. Invite him to shape your Up, In, and Out relationships. When you live this way, you will take the Kingdom of God with you wherever you go. And wherever you go, look for persons of peace (cf. Luke 10). Persons of peace are those who like you, listen to you, and serve you. Share Kingdom life with them. Share the good news of the Kingdom with them so they might respond and enter into God's Kingdom, too.

Explore how *The Triangle* can help you live a life full of deeper relationships.

THE TRIANGLE: DEEPER RELATIONSHIPS

THE MAIN IDEA:

Jesus models and invites us to live out three-dimensional lives of up, in, and out relationships.

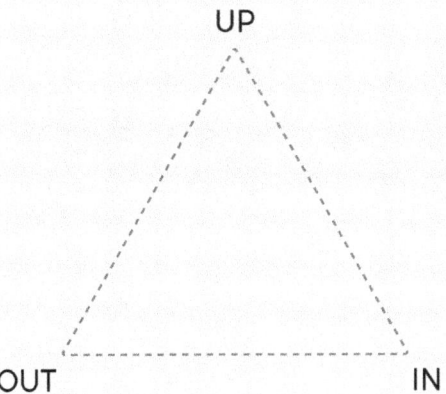

UP

OUT   IN

BUILD THE TRIANGLE:

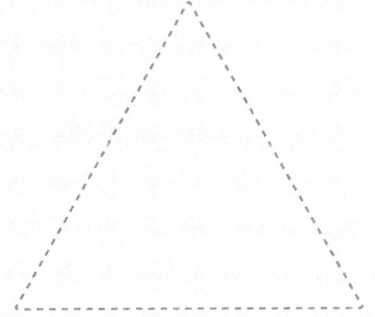

STUDY QUESTIONS

1. In your own words, define Up, In, and Out.

Up -

In -

Out -

2. Of Up, In, and Out, which comes most naturally to you? Which comes least naturally?

3. How does your church balance all three dimensions of Up, In, and Out? If it doesn't, how does your church express itself - as an Up and Inner church, an Up and Outer Church or an In and Outer church?

4. Consider your relationships. Are you looking for and responding to persons of peace? If so, what's the next step in that relationship? If not, how could you create space to begin looking for the persons of peace God is placing in your life?

5

THE SEMI-CIRCLE: RHYTHM OF LIFE

Building a Discipling Culture: Chapter 9

God created us to work, but does this mean that we are to be workaholics? Even though many in ministry and life burnout from working too much, it does not have to be this way. Stress-filled work isn't just something chosen by those in Christian life and ministry either; it's prevalent in the lives of everyone. As people in a fallen world, we more often than not build our identity around our activities or work. We aren't human *doings*, though. We are human *beings*!

God shows us that the pattern of rest and work is rooted in the story of Adam and Eve before the fall. As humanity, our first experience as created beings with our Creator God is a day of rest. To fulfill our calling to be fruitful, we must start from a place of rest: be-to-do *not* do-to-be.

Resting in God -- abiding in his presence -- is the only way we can be successful in what he has called us to do. The call to rest is so essential to fruitful lives as human beings that God includes it in his Top Ten (the ten commandments) that includes, "don't kill," "don't steal," and "don't commit murder." Rest matters!

Jesus teaches the same principle in John 15 in the illustration of the vine and the branches. He teaches the disciples that to bear fruit, they must grow, and to grow, they must abide (or rest) in him.

While we are all called to rest, *how* we rest depends on how God creates us. For example, introverts and extroverts rest differently, and that is okay! Reflect on what gives you rest and don't feel guilty if it looks different than others. Just remember, resting is not being lazy. It's taking the time to "recharge" and abide in God. Resting is also not something we do irregularly. Be sure to build rhythms of rest into every day, week, month, and season. Continually look at examples of rest in Jesus' life to imitate him (cf. Mark 1:12-13; 1:35-39; 6:30-32). As the pendulum of life swings from rest to work and back again, by staying grounded in Christ, he will produce growth and fruit in your life.

Where are you currently at on the pendulum between work and rest? Use *The Semi-Circle* to live a balanced rhythm of life.

THE SEMI-CIRCLE: RHYTHM OF LIFE

THE MAIN IDEA:

God created humanity to work from a place of rest, and disciples find their rest as they abide in Jesus.

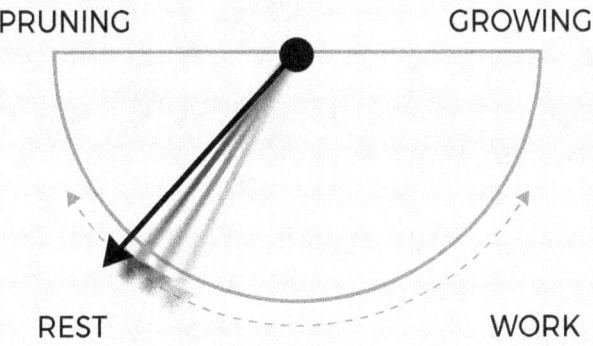

BUILD THE SEMI-CIRCLE:

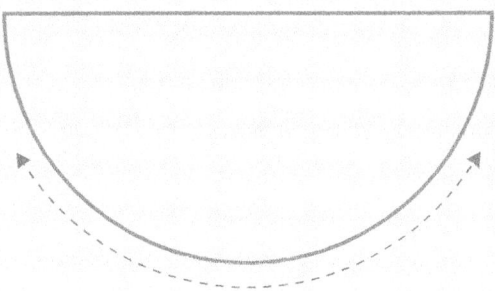

STUDY QUESTIONS

1. Identify examples of rest and work in Jesus' life and ministry:

    Rest -

    Work -

2. Ponder on the last time you experienced burnout or something close to it. What were the factors in your life that led you to burnout?

3. Are you currently in a season of abiding (rest), pruning (growth), or fruitfulness (work)? How does it show?

4. Compare Jesus' model of rest and work to your own patterns of rest and work. How could you improve your situation by following Jesus' teaching in John 15?

5. Begin to dream about what predictable patterns of rest might look like in your life. What patterns of rest could you have daily? Weekly? Monthly? Seasonally? Annually?

6

THE SQUARE: MULTIPLYING LIFE

Building a Discipling Culture: Chapter 10

Jesus' leadership style is dramatically different than the leadership style of our culture and as a part of it the Church. The broader culture has developed into a management-oriented society. Jesus' leadership culture is not about managing growth, productivity, or human resources. Instead, in Mark 10:42-45, the evangelist quotes Jesus as saying the opposite to the twelve,

> You know that those who are regarded as rulers of the Gentiles lord it over them, and their high officials exercise authority over them. Not so with you. Instead, whoever wants to become great among you must be your servant, and whoever wants to be first must be slave of all. For even the Son of Man did not come to be served, but to serve, and to give his life as a ransom for many.

Jesus' words speak as directly into our culture today as they did when he first said them. Our leadership should model Jesus' leadership, which is not about position, but about how we relate to one another. The Church needs leaders who will choose not to manage the Church, but choose to be disciples who train others with the tools they need to make disciples. To make disciples-who-make-disciples requires a high degree of accessibility to the life of a leader. This leader must understand what is needed for each stage of development. Jesus is a master at this.

In Jesus' leadership, we see four stages. In each of those stages, the disciple is growing in varying expressions of confidence and competence. To serve them best, Jesus matches his leadership style to what each disciple needs most at that stage of their development. The LifeShape of *The Square* helps easily recall the following principles. Each phase of leadership (or side of *The Square*) leads to the next.

- **Stage One:** The disciple is confident and incompetent (D1), so the leadership style is directive (L1).
- **Stage Two:** The disciple is unenthusiastic and incompetent (D2), so the leadership style is visionary/coach (L2).
- **Stage Three:** The disciple is growing in confidence (D3), so the leadership style is pastoral/consensus (L3).
- **Stage Four:** The end of disciple's development is in sight (D4), so the leadership style is delegation (D4).

Another way of describing these four stages is:

- **Stage One:** I do, you watch
- **Stage Two:** I do, you help
- **Stage Three:** You do, I help
- **Stage Four:** You do, I watch

The goal of Jesus' ministry is not to just make disciples, but to make disciples-who-make-disciples. He does this by inviting them to walk with him every step of the way and by increasing the challenge of responsibility until they are ready to carry on the ministry without him. Use *The Square* in your life and ministry to multiply disciples.

THE SQUARE: MULTIPLYING LIFE

THE MAIN IDEA:

To lead like Jesus is to disciple people through intentional relationships to grow in Christlikeness until they are leading others to do the same.

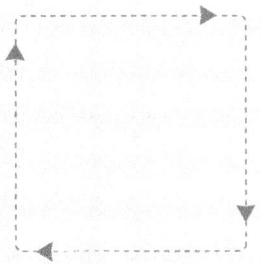

L_1/D_1
I Do, You Watch

L_4/D_4
You Do, I Watch

L_2/D_2
I Do, You Help

L_3/D_3
You Do, I Help

BUILD THE SQUARE:

STUDY QUESTIONS

1. Consider Jesus' words in Mark 10:42-45. He gives a strong correction to his disciples when he says, "Not so with you." How does this speak into or against current approaches to leadership?

2. Describe what you see in your church's current leadership culture. Is it patterned after our culture's management-oriented leadership or Jesus' relationship-oriented leadership? How so?

3. Which of the four styles of leadership comes most naturally and least naturally for you -- directive; visionary/coach; pastoral/consensus; delegation?

4. What could go wrong in leading others with the inappropriate style of leadership for whatever stage of discipleship they might be at? How will it look when you lead people appropriately?

5. Write down an honest sassessment of your current leadership of others. What steps can you take toward building a Christ-like leadership character?

7

THE PENTAGON: PERSONAL CALLING

Building a Discipling Culture: Chapter 11

Cultural consumerism holds profound influence in the life of the Church, laying a heavy burden on a few that often leads to burnout. Yes, there are roles within the Church, but the call to mission is given to every disciple. Healthy churches build discipling cultures where all members are trained to participate in the mission of God.

Christ gives a diversity of gifts to the Church and to all her members for this mission. The role of church leaders is to help disciples discover, develop, and deliver their spiritual gifts. Several New Testament passages speak of gifts for the Church, including 1 Corinthians 12, Romans 12, 1 Peter 4, and Ephesians 4. Upon further investigation, you will find that the former three are written to specific communities, whereas Ephesians 4 is something like a memo of sorts to many churches. Consider Paul's words in Ephesians 4:7, 11-13:

> But to each one of us grace has been given as Christ apportioned it. So Christ himself gave the apostles, the prophets, the evange-lists, the pastors and teachers, to equip his people for works of

service, so that the body of Christ may be built up until we all reach unity in the faith and in the knowledge of the Son of God and become mature, attaining to the whole measure of the fullness of Christ.

Here are some helpful definitions that we've found useful:

- **Apostle**: From the Greek *apostolos* meaning "one who is sent out," apostles are visionary and pioneering, always pushing into new territory.

- **Prophet**: One who hears and listens to God (*prophetes*); the prophet foretells and tells forth revelation from God.

- **Evangelist**: One who brings good news and shares the message readily (*euangellistes*); the evangelist loves to spend time with non-Christians and remind other Christians that there are non-Christians still in the world.

- **Pastor**: One who shepherds God's people (*poimen*); shepherds care for others with a tender heart, see needs, provide comfort, and encourage others.

- **Teacher**: One who holds forth the truth and is excited by it (*didaskalos*); teachers look for ways to explain, enlighten, and apply truth.

Working together in unity (Eph 4:1-6), these five gifts are apportioned by Christ to each disciple in the Church, with everyone relying on one another as the Church carries out God's mission. Each one of us has a **base ministry** that represents one of the fivefold ministries in Ephesians. However, there are times and seasons when God leads us to discover the other ministries for a brief time -- this is a **phase ministry**. Having a phase ministry allows us to be well rounded, both personally and as a body. As Paul says it, we "become mature."

So how do you discover your base ministry? First ask yourself if you are a pioneer or a settler/developer. Pioneers love pushing into new territory and helping to create breakthrough. Settlers and developers are the steady, solid backbone of most communities. In ministry terms (generally speaking), the pioneers would be Apostles, Prophets, and Evangelists. Pastors and Teachers tend to be of the developer nature. Another way to discover your base ministry is to ask your community what they think while using a helpful tool like the Fivefold Ministries Questionnaire at www.fivefoldsurvey.com.

As you discover your own gifting and lead others to discover theirs, remember we must not box anyone into an identity or expression they are not comfortable with. Testing comes into our lives to make us more flexible, though. God stretches us by taking us into new territory, by moving us into new phases of ministry. This leads to our maturity in our base gifting and our unity as the Body of Christ. Use *The Pentagon* to help identify your base gifting and help navigate your phase ministry.

THE PENTAGON: PERSONAL CALLING

THE MAIN IDEA:

Christ apportions the gifts of Apostles, Prophets, Evangelists, Pastors, and Teachers to the church for its maturity and unity in mission.

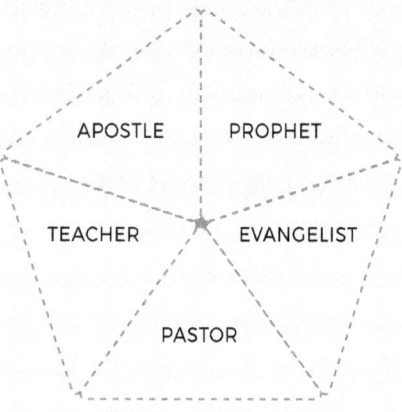

BUILD THE PENTAGON:

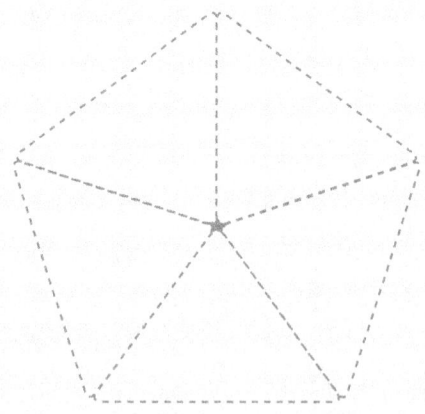

STUDY QUESTIONS

1. What has been your experience with spiritual gifts in the Church?

2. How do you see the fivefold ministry on display in Jesus' life?

3.   Take the Fivefold Ministry Survey. What are your thoughts on the results of your base ministry? Ask another follower of Jesus what they think is your fivefold base ministry.

4.   How are you currently operating in your base ministry, or perhaps, in your phase ministry?

5. What would it look like right now if others in your church worked together in your shared ministries? If you aren't opperating out of the fivefild ministry, what could be your first step?

8

THE HEXAGON: DEFINITIVE PRAYER

Building a Discipling Culture: Chapter 12

The disciples spent most all their time with Jesus, learning from him by watching him. Jesus spent a lot of his time with his Father in prayer. On one occasion, reflecting on Jesus' unique way of praying, the disciples asked, "Lord, teach us to pray." In response, Jesus does not give the disciples several modes to choose from, but a singular model that summarizes his Kingdom way of life. We commonly know this prayer as the Lord's Prayer.

> Our Father in heaven, hallowed be your name, (Character)
> Your Kingdom come, your will be done on earth as it is in heaven.
> (Kingdom)
> Give us today our daily bread. (Provision)
> Forgive us our debts, as we also have forgiven our debtors. (Forgiveness)
> And lead us not into temptation, (Guidance)
> but deliver us from the evil one. (Protection)
>
> Matthew 6:9-13

Praying these six phrases, or aspects, of the Lord's Prayer plants the seed of the Kingdom in our hearts that, when nourished, will bear fruit in our leadership of others and our walk with God.

Slow down and study each section of the prayer. As you do so, you will find a framework in which every corner of your life is addressed. You might begin by praying each phrase word-for-word, giving pause so that your cares and concerns fill the space that phrase created.

Picture the prayer as the filling of a bottle, where each of your requests drops into the bottle and is held together by the prayer. Or you can picture the prayer as a bottle poured out over each of your requests, where the Lord's Prayer covers each of your requests.

This is just the beginning of a prayer life led and directed by the Lord's Prayer. There is no end to the influence that the Lord's Prayer might have on your life. Your prayers will take on an ever-growing shape and substance as you move from the Lord's Prayer being something you learn how to recite to something that continually takes you into deeper communication with the Father.

THE HEXAGON: DEFINITIVE PRAYER

THE MAIN IDEA:

In the Lord's Prayer, Jesus gives us the definitive model for communing with and communicating to the Father.

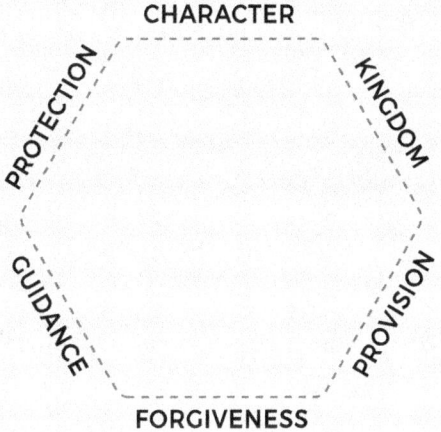

BUILD THE HEXAGON:

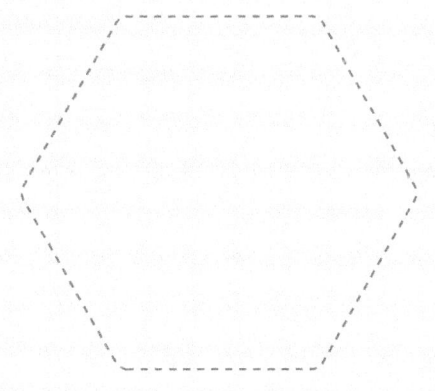

STUDY QUESTIONS

1. Diverse expressions of prayer in the Church are deeply rooted in the Lord's Prayer. Describe your exposure to and experience with the Lord's Prayer. Has it been neutral, positive, or negative?

2. How does Jesus' teaching on prayer continually reshape your view of God?

3. Slow down and consider each of the aspects of this prayer and rate
    yourself from 1-10 on how it each informs your prayer life. What is
    abundant? What is lacking? Why do you think that is?

    Character –

    Kingdom –

    Provision –

    Forgiveness –

    Guidance –

    Protection –

4. In the space below, write down needs, requests, or ideas that come to mind with each of the six aspects of the Lord's Prayer. Take time to pray through what you wrote down as you go throughout your week.

    Character –

    Kingdom –

    Provision –

    Forgiveness –

    Guidance –

    Protection –

9

HUDDLE

Building a Discipling Culture: Part 3

Part 3 of *Building a Discipling Culture* gives further insight into how to use the vehicle of Huddles. Huddles are a place to directly disciple your current or future leaders in mission and discipleship through regular encouragement and accountability.

Huddles are not small groups. Small groups tend to be open to everyone and grow when you add new people. Huddles are open to current and future leaders and grow when current members start a Huddle of their own. You can read more about the difference between Huddles and small groups in *Building a Discipling Culture*, but most of all remember this: often the purpose of small groups is addition while the purpose of Huddles is multiplication. What we mean by this is that Huddles are designed to make disciples who make disciples, while often small groups remain stuck in a model where leaders always stay leaders, and small group participants sometimes, if ever, become leaders. Huddles are about cultivating a culture of disciple-making disciples.

In an opening note on Part 3 of *Building a Discipling Culture*, Mike writes, "One other caveat I'd like to make: My advice is to resist the urge to start a Huddle because you've read the material on how to lead one. The only way to lead a Huddle successfully is to first be in one."

After years of practice and reflection, Mike Breen and his team have recognized that emerging generations, influenced by emerging technologies, maintain their relationships through *asynchronous* relationships ("at different times"). Whether it's texting, social media apps, or new ways of communicating like Marco Polo, Voxer, or texting, people are talking with each other today in ways that don't require *synchronistic* forms of communication ("at the same time"). Huddles are primarily about relationships that form and reproduce disciples. The timing of Huddles can be either *synchronistic* or *asynchronistic*.

To foster discipleship and development using this growing asynchronistic expression of communication, Mike and his team have launched *The Missional Institute*: https://missionalinstitute.com/.

So if you desire to learn how to Huddle others but don't have someone to teach you, learn how to make disciples using the Huddle directly from those who have re-discovered this missional vehicle.

In a *Missional Institute* Huddle, you will experience regular asynchronistic reflection and coaching through the *LifeShapes* you've learned about in *Building a Discipling Culture*. Even more, your participation in the *Missional Institute* will train, empower, and give you an online and asynchronistic vehicle to begin Huddles of your own. Just like the Huddles described in *Building a Discipling Culture*, you will learn how to reflect through your experiences in disciple-making while asking the two imporant questions for every area of life: "What is God saying to me?" and "What am I going to do about it?"

We will train you in a *Missional Institute* Huddle in each of the *LifeShapes* by a trusted coach. And more than anything, you will be formed as a disciples able to easily start your own Huddles using the same vehicles you have experienced in a way that leads to multiplication.